A Hard Day's Work

Story by
Mick Gowar

Pictures by
Margaret Chamberlain

DELACORTE PRESS/NEW YORK

Published by
Delacorte Press
Bantam Doubleday Dell Publishing Group, Inc.
666 Fifth Avenue
New York, New York 10103

This work was originally published in Great Britain
by André Deutsch Limited.

Library of Congress Cataloging-in- Publication Data

Gowar, Mick, 1951–
  A hard day's work.

  Summary: A little girl spends the day with Dad in his office and wreaks havoc.
  [1. Fathers — Fiction]   I. Chamberlain, Margaret,
ill.   II. Title.

PZ7.G747Har   1989   [E]   88-18908
ISBN 0 385-29763-7

Manufactured in Italy

    October 1989
10 9 8 7 6 5 4 3 2 1

One day when Mom was feeling sick and Grandma was on vacation a long way away, Dad said I could go to work with him . . . if I promised to be very, very good.

We went to the city on a train.

There were a lot of people on the train
so there wasn't much room for running.

Dad works in a very tall building. We got into an elevator.

Dad's friend Eric was in the elevator. I pressed all the buttons.

The elevator went up and down . . . and up and down . . . and up and down.

I don't think Eric liked the elevator but I did.

In Dad's office there were lots of buttons to press on the phone
. . . on the typewriter
. . . on the computer.

Dad showed me how to work the computer. You have to put round flat things in it. I tried when Dad was talking to Eric. I wasn't very good at doing it.

Dad's friend Eric looked a bit angry. They had a cup of coffee and I ate lots of chocolate cookies. I sat at a big desk and did some coloring in my coloring book.

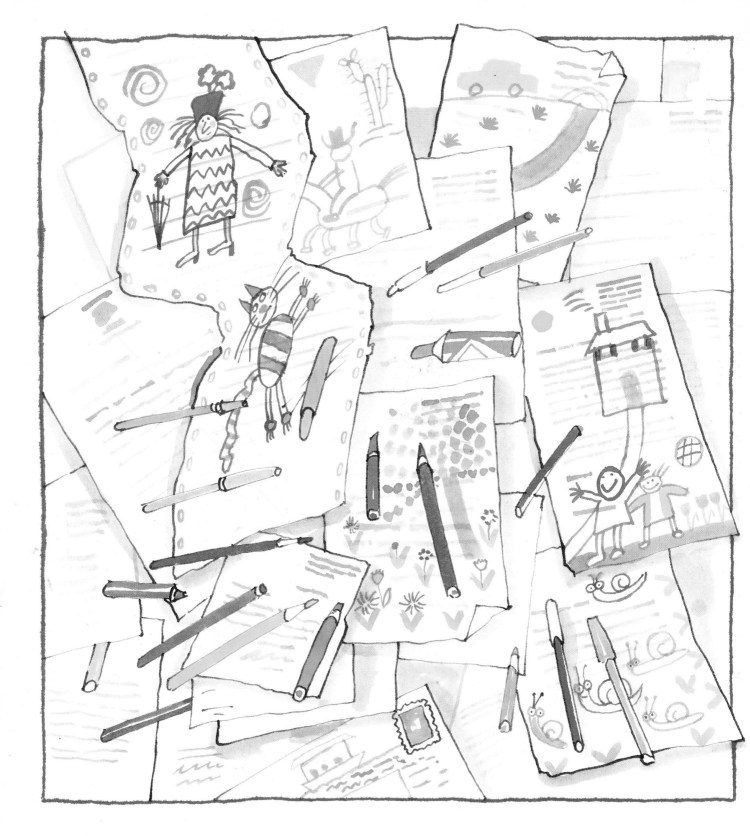

Then I drew some pictures on some other paper and colored those.

Dad's friend Eric got angry again . . .

so I played hiding-in-the- closet.

There were lots of things to play with in the closet.
Nobody found me for a very long time.

After washing my hands I went exploring. I played lions-under-the-table.

I am a very fierce lion. I can bite very hard.

I frightened an old man who was sitting at the table.

Dad looked frightened too.

I was very good for ages and ages. I found some scissors.

I am very good at cutting things.

Dad's friend Eric was angry again. So was Dad.

He said, "We'd better go home now."

We said good-bye to everybody.

The old man was in the elevator. Dad *didn't* let me push the buttons.

When we got home Mom was feeling better,
but *Dad* was feeling sick.
So Mom got up and made my supper and Dad got into bed.

Tomorrow I'm going to work with Mom.